For Benjamin, of course! R.L.

For Atha Tehon, Art Director —
my work is always enhanced by her light touch. S.J.

Published by Dial Books for Young Readers
A Division of Penguin Books USA Inc.
375 Hudson Street · New York, New York 10014

Published simultaneously in Canada by
Fitzhenry & Whiteside Limited, Toronto
Text copyright © 1990 by Reeve Lindbergh
Pictures copyright © 1990 by Susan Jeffers
All rights reserved
Printed in the U.S.A.
Design by Atha Tehon
First Edition
E
1 3 5 7 9 10 8 6 4 2

Library of Congress Cataloging in Publication Data
Lindbergh, Reeve.
Benjamin's barn / written by Reeve Lindbergh
illustrated by Susan Jeffers.
p.   cm.
Summary: Describes in verse Benjamin's magnificent barn,
which is enormously warm, tall, wide, soft, clean, and full.
ISBN 0-8037-0613-8.   ISBN 0-8037-0614-6 (lib. bdg.)
[1. Barns — Fiction. 2. Farm life — Fiction. 3. Stories in rhyme.]
I. Jeffers, Susan, ill. II. Title.
PZ8.3.L6148Be 1990   [E] — dc19   88-23690   CIP   AC

Benjamin's Barn

REEVE LINDBERGH

paintings *by* SUSAN JEFFERS

Dial Books for Young Readers · New York

Benjamin's barn
Is so big and so warm
He could shelter an elephant
Safe from a storm

Or nestle a lamb
That's just barely been born
(Because Benjamin's barn
Is enormously warm).

Benjamin's barn
Is so big and so tall
He could hide a whole pirate ship there —
Mast and all!

Or an old piebald horse
In a high-ceilinged stall
(Because Benjamin's barn
Is enormously tall).

Benjamin's barn
Is so big and so wide
He could easily keep
Pterodactyls inside

Or a dozen plump pigeons
Arranged side by side
(Because Benjamin's barn
Is enormously wide).

Benjamin's barn
Is so big and so soft
He could ask a frail princess
To sleep in the trough

Or a pair of raccoons
To curl up in the loft
(Because Benjamin's barn
Is enormously soft).

Benjamin's barn
Is so big and so grand
He could call up the mayor
To send a brass band

Or just have ten geese
And a gander on hand
(Because Benjamin's barn
Is enormously grand).

Benjamin's barn
Is so big and so clean
He could hold a great ball
For the king and the queen

Or the cow and the bull
And the milking machine
(Because Benjamin's barn
Is enormously clean).

Benjamin's barn
Is so big and so neat
He could toss a rhinoceros in
For a treat

Or a bossy old billygoat
Quick on his feet
(Because Benjamin's barn
Is enormously neat).

But…Benjamin's barn
Is so big and so full
With the horse, cow, goat, pigeons,
Raccoons, sheep, geese, bull,

That he thinks he won't ask the rest in
After all
(Because Benjamin's barn
Is enormously full)!